GAZELLE

KATE'S SKATES

by

BEVERLEY MATHIAS

Illustrated by Rob Chapman

HAMISH HAMILTON

LONDON

For Katherine with love

HAMISH HAMILTON LTD

Published by the Penguin Group
27 Wrights Lane, London w8 5TZ, England
Viking Penguin Inc, 40 West 23rd Street, New York, New York 10010, U.S.A.
Penguin Books Australia Ltd, Ringwood, Victoria, Australia
Penguin Books Canada Ltd, 2801 John Street, Markham, Ontario, Canada L3R 1B4
Penguin Books (N.Z.) Ltd, 182-190 Wairau Road, Auckland 10, New Zealand

Penguin Books Ltd, Registered Offices: Harmondsworth, Middlesex, England

First published in Great Britain 1990 by
Hamish Hamilton Ltd

Text copyright © 1990 by Beverley Mathias
Illustrations copyright © 1990 by Rob Chapman

1 3 5 7 9 10 8 6 4 2

British Library Cataloguing in Publication Data
CIP data for this book is available from the British Library

ISBN 0-241-12750-5

Printed in Great Britain at the University Press, Cambridge

Chapter One

Kate and Drew were twins, and they lived with Mum and Dad in a big white house in the country. Dad was an officer in the Navy and they lived on the base. The beach was just down the hill, there wasn't much traffic, and kangaroos and wallabies came right up to the house.

There was just one problem. Kate and Drew didn't mind the fifty-mile ride to school each day, but they did mind not being able to go roller-

skating. Kate loved roller-skating.
When she was six, Grandma had
given her a pair of roller-skates for her
birthday. That was before they moved
from Sydney to the country. Kate had
become quite a good skater, and she
loved going to the roller-skating rink.
But now they lived on the base, Mum
and Dad wouldn't let her skate alone
outside because of the hills. The
house was on the edge of a cliff and all
the paths sloped towards the beach.
Her skates were getting old and
battered and almost too small, but
Kate knew she wouldn't get new ones
until Mum and Dad felt it was safe
and she wouldn't do anything silly on
the hilly paths. Kate wished that they
could skate in the nice, flat car-park,

but the Navy wouldn't allow it. Dad said it was a sensible rule, but Kate and Drew thought there was enough room for the cars and roller-skating *and* football, if everyone was careful. So Kate took her skates to school and skated in the playground at lunchtime and after school, while they waited for Mum to finish teaching and take them home. Sometimes in the holidays Mum took them to the rink in the next town as a special treat. The floor was much smoother than the playground.

Now it was school holidays and Kate couldn't skate at all. Mum was away from home at a teachers' conference and Dad had to go to the office every morning, so Kate and

Drew were feeling bored. Drew wouldn't have minded going to the beach to paddle and build sandcastles, but Kate just wanted to go roller-skating.

They sat at the breakfast table and watched Dad make toast. Kate looked at Drew, then said, "Dad, could you take the day off today and take us roller-skating . . . please?"

"No, Kate," said Dad, "you know I must go to the office every morning, and it's too far to drive to the rink after lunch."

"It's not fair, why do we have to stay home? Mum should be here. Why did she have to go to that stupid conference anyway?" moaned Kate.

"You know Mum really wanted to

go, and you said you didn't mind," reminded Dad. "Anyway, she'll be home in two days' time. Perhaps she'll take you roller-skating next week."

Drew nudged Kate and smiled, but Kate just turned her back and sulked.

Dad looked at them both. "Now, listen you two. This morning you're going to stay with Mrs Robinson and she said she would take you out. I'll give you some money in case you stay out for lunch. Make sure you behave, and you can tell me about it when you come home."

Chapter Two

Kate and Drew finished their breakfast and went to their rooms. Drew packed his jumper, a book and a ball in his schoolbag. Kate stood in front of the mirror and looked at her new front tooth. Last week there had just been a big gap waiting for two new teeth, but the day after Mum left one new tooth had begun to appear and now it was all there. Kate was proud of her new tooth. Drew hadn't even lost his first teeth yet, so he didn't have any gaps. As well as her new front tooth, Kate had three more gaps waiting for new teeth to grow into them.

"Come on," shouted Drew down the passage. "Put your things in a bag and let's go and find out where Mrs Robinson is taking us."

"I don't want to," said Kate. "You go and find out."

Drew ran across the grass to Mrs Robinson's house. She lived next door and often babysat when the twins' parents were out. She heard Drew coming and opened the back door.

"Hello Drew, where's Kate?" she asked.

"Kate's home sulking," replied Drew. "She wants to go roller-skating and Dad won't take us because it's too far to go after lunch."

"That's a pity," said Mrs Robinson. "About Kate sulking, I mean. Because roller-skating is where we *are* going. I know it's a long drive to the rink, but your father said we could go for the day."

Drew's eyes opened wide and his face split into a delighted grin.

"Oh, that's great. I'll go and tell Kate. What time do you want us to be ready?" He jumped up and down on the spot with excitement.

"Calm down," laughed Mrs Robinson. "I haven't even done the breakfast dishes yet. Be over here in half an hour."

Kate was sitting on her bed,

brushing her hair. Drew burst into
her room and shouted, "Guess what!
Mrs Robinson is taking us roller-
skating and Dad says we can go."

Kate looked at Drew to make sure
he was telling the truth and then she
began to smile. Her grin got wider

9

and wider. She bounced on the bed. "Yippee!" she yelled. "Quick, let me get my things ready."

They both giggled as Kate stuffed a jumper, a book and her purse into a bag. She looked at what she was wearing and wondered if she should wear her special skating skirt. She found her skates and a clean pair of long white socks. Suddenly she stood stock-still and began to dream of all the wonderful things she would do on her skates.

"Come on," said Drew. "Stop dreaming."

Kate picked up her bag and stuffed her skating skirt inside. Then, with her skates in the other hand, she followed Drew to the kitchen where

Dad was doing the dishes.

"You knew all the time, didn't you?" said Kate to Dad.

"I might have," teased Dad. "Now, here's some money each for lunch, and extra money for hiring skates for Drew. Don't spend it all on sweets, and try to remember to buy Mrs Robinson a cup of tea. Have a nice day. I'll see you about five o'clock."

Kate and Drew kissed Dad goodbye, picked up their bags and ran out of the house.

Chapter Three

"There you are," said Mrs Robinson, as the twins came running across the grass. "Sit here and mind my bag."

Kate and Drew sat on the front steps with Mrs Robinson's bag, their own two bags and Kate's skates. They waited as Mrs Robinson backed the car out of the garage. Then they climbed into the back and put their bags and the skates on the floor.

"Don't forget to belt up," reminded Mrs Robinson. But Kate and Drew had already buckled up their seat-belts.

First they went to get petrol. Then they drove out of the base and onto the main road. Mrs Robinson handed Drew a map and said, "You will have to guide me once we reach Moombarigah because I'm not sure where the skating rink is."

"Oh, we know where it is," said Kate, "and Drew's very good at reading maps."

First they drove along narrow country roads before turning onto the busy main road which led to the town. Drew and Kate told jokes and read their books until Kate began to fidget. Then the scenery changed and they could see lots of houses, shops

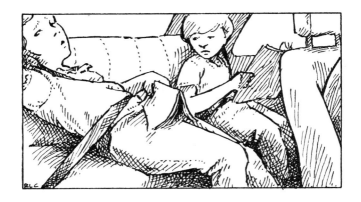

and other buildings.

"We're nearly there now," said Mrs
Robinson. "Drew, could you look at
the map please and tell me where I
have to turn?"

Drew watched the street signs and
the map carefully, directing Mrs
Robinson to 'turn left' and 'turn
right'. Soon they were in the middle of
Moombarigah, and Kate saw a sign
which said 'Roller-Skating Rink'.

"There! There!" she shouted, bouncing up and down on the seat.

"Shut up!" said Drew. "I know the sign says that way, but it's better to go this way because it goes straight into the car-park."

Drew directed Mrs Robinson around the corner away from the sign, then around two more corners. In front of them was the entrance to the car-park and beyond that, behind all the cars, was the skating rink with people going in and out of the doors.

Kate wriggled around in her seatbelt, trying to pick up all her things so that she could get out of the car quickly.

"Kate," said Mrs Robinson, "slow down. You can't go without us, and you must wait until I have stopped the car properly before you get out."

Kate was so excited she felt she couldn't wait another minute without bursting. All the time she skated in the playground at school, she thought about going to the rink and being able to skate without tripping over stones. Now she was here at last, and she felt the next few minutes were going to take forever. Even after they got out of the car, Kate knew she would have to wait for Drew, then wait for a ticket, and wait until she had her skates on. It seemed that she would never get onto the rink.

Mrs Robinson ignored Kate's fidgets and parked the car. They gathered their things together and

18

waited while Mrs Robinson locked
up. Finally they walked across the
car-park to the roller-skating rink.

Chapter Four

Kate and Drew stopped inside the
entrance and felt around in their bags
for the money Dad had given them.

"It's OK," said Mrs Robinson,
"this is my treat. You can buy your
own lunch."

"Thanks – we could buy your
lunch, too," they both replied.

Mrs Robinson laughed. "You don't
have to do that, but a cup of tea
would be nice."

They queued up and waited to pay.

Drew paid to hire skates as well. Once they were through the turnstile, Mrs Robinson looked around for somewhere to buy a drink. Kate showed her where the drink machines were and they each chose something.

They took their drinks and sat down where they could see the rink. Kate thought some of the children were quite good, but some seemed to be always falling over. A man came onto the rink and spoke to some children who were skating very fast across the middle of the floor.

"You're not allowed to do that," said Kate. "You have to keep to the edge and leave the middle for people who want to practise turns and jumps."

They finished their drinks and picked up their bags. "I'll go and wait for you beside the rink," said Mrs Robinson. "You go and get ready."

Kate and Drew went towards the hire shop. Kate stopped to look in the window of the rink shop and saw they had some skates just like the ones she wanted. They were white leather with proper supports and a jump bar. The bearings were fully positioned and Kate knew that they would be much better than the skates she now used. Her old skates were just sneakers. They had stoppers, but Dad had to keep replacing the bearings because they only lasted about three months. These lovely white leather boots had bearings which were much better

and would probably last a year.
She looked at the price. They were
expensive and would take a lot of
pocket money. Perhaps she could ask
Grandma for money for her birthday
and Christmas, but it would still
mean saving all the money she had.

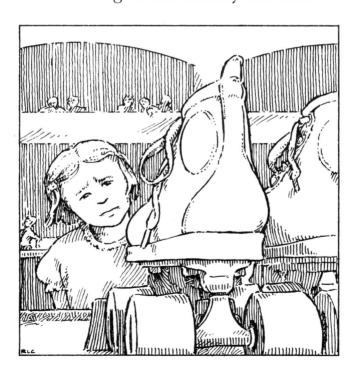

Kate went into the changing room and changed into her skating skirt, clean socks and her skates. When Drew reappeared she was looking at the skates again.

"Come on, Kate," he said. "Stop dreaming about new skates. You know Dad won't buy them because you've got nowhere to use them. Let's go out onto the rink."

Kate heaved a great sigh and followed Drew down to where Mrs Robinson was sitting. She put her things down and went with Drew out onto the rink. It was a good floor, wooden and very smooth. Kate knew she was going to enjoy herself. She warmed up first by skating round the edge with Drew a few times, then waved to him and went into the middle. It was no good imagining that the white leather boots were on her feet. She knew she was wearing dirty old sneaker-skates, but she still felt good.

After skating round, practising her inside edge, she decided to try the backwards crossover she had read about in a skating magazine. She thought about it first. "Left foot crosses behind right foot, be careful of the edges." She skated backwards carefully and did the step successfully. She did it three more times, then skated forwards and turned a full circle on her right foot with her left foot held out behind. Her confidence growing, she thought about trying a

jump. That was much more difficult, but she had watched and watched the good skaters and she thought she could do it. A free jump might be best, so she skated off on her left foot, jumped with a half turn in the air and landed on her right foot. Kate felt pleased and did it again, then she tried skating on her right foot and landing on her left. That worked too – and she hadn't fallen once.

Drew watched Kate from where he was skating around the edge. He was quite happy going round and round, sometimes fast and sometimes slow, but he didn't have the confidence of Kate to try jumps and turns. He did like watching her and he could see that she was getting much better as she jumped. He watched her jumping first from one foot and then the other and showing off to the other children. Then he saw her stand still. She seemed to be thinking.

Kate *was* thinking. She had just seen a big girl do a single-axel jump. The girl had jumped into the air and turned right round before landing on her right foot. Then she did a double-axel and turned before landing on both feet. Kate thought it looked easy – landing on two feet must be much easier than landing on one, and she could already do that. She skated off, still thinking about the axel jump.

"Skate fast on my left foot, then jump and turn around in the air and land on my right foot," thought Kate. "Or I could jump off both feet and land on both feet."

She decided to try a double-axel first and skated carefully in a circle. She skated a bit faster and jumped, turning in the air and coming down on both feet. Kate grinned to herself. Then she did it again, but this time she jumped a bit higher. Feeling very pleased, Kate decided to try a single-axel jump and skated off fast so she would have enough speed to jump from one foot. She jumped from her left foot, turned in the air and missed her footing. She wobbled, her skates went from under her and she landed on her face, sliding along the floor.

Drew was watching and saw her

fall. He waited, but she didn't get up. He was frightened and skated quickly into the middle of the rink.

"Are you all right?" he called out to Kate. "Can you get up?"

Kate just lay there. Some big girls and boys skated up.

"Can you help me, please? I think my sister's hurt," said Drew.

They looked at Kate. She wasn't crying, and she didn't seem to be hurt, but then she lifted her face and Drew saw the blood pouring out of her mouth.

"What's happened, Kate?" he said. "Is your mouth cut?"

Kate shook her head and looked very scared, but she didn't say anything, or open her mouth.

The older children helped Kate to the edge of the rink. Mrs Robinson hurried over to them, looking worried.

"What have you done, Kate?" she asked. "Drew, you'd better go and find the first-aid person." Mrs Robinson thanked the others and they went back onto the rink.

Drew went off, still with his skates on, to find the first-aid room. Soon he was back with a man who was carrying a large case. He put it on the seat and sat down next to Kate.

"Now, let's have a look at what you've done, young lady," he said kindly.

Kate opened her mouth. At first the man couldn't see anything wrong, but when he looked again he said, "Did you have a front tooth?"

Mrs Robinson looked in Kate's mouth. "Oh Kate, your beautiful new tooth, it's broken."

Kate began to cry. Her new front tooth! Mum hadn't even seen it, and now it was broken.

The man turned to Drew and said, "While I'm trying to help your sister, why don't you go back onto the rink and see if you can find the missing piece of tooth."

Drew skated off. Some of the other children came to help, but it was no use. They couldn't find the missing piece.

The first-aid man mopped up the blood in Kate's mouth with some cotton wool and very carefully touched the broken tooth. "It's not going to fall out, but you must have hit the floor very hard to break off such a big piece. I think you should go to your dentist. He will know what to do."

Kate nodded, the tears running down her face. She had been so pleased with her new tooth, and now it was broken. She knew it was her own fault . . . she shouldn't really have been trying to jump, and Dad would be very angry with her.

Mrs Robinson thanked the first-aid man as Drew came off the rink. They gathered up their things. Mrs Robinson helped Kate out of her skates and into her shoes while Drew went off to return his skates to the hire shop. Sadly they walked out of the building and across to the car. They were all very quiet. Mrs Robinson didn't know what she was going to say to the twins' father. He was going to be very upset when he saw Kate.

Once they were safely in the car,

Mrs Robinson said, "Kate, we'll go to the dentist straight away. Do you know his name?"

"He's not in this town," said Drew. "He's near where we go to school, but I can't remember where."

There was nothing for it but to return home and sadly they set off.

Chapter Five

All the way home Kate thought about
her tooth. Her mouth hurt – in fact
she hurt all over from falling on the
floor of the rink. She knew she would
have bruises tomorrow, but worst of
all was her broken tooth. It had been
silly to show off and try to do those
difficult steps, but Kate wanted to
show the other children how good she
was. Now she hurt and her lovely new
tooth was broken in half. Despite
feeling sorry for herself and guilty

36

because she hadn't been more careful,
Kate still wanted to skate. She felt she
would be able to skate much better
with proper skates, like the ones in the
rink shop, but there wasn't much
chance of that now.

Drew tried to cheer her up, but she
didn't want to talk, or laugh at his
jokes. She just sat hunched up in the
corner, held in by her seatbelt.

They rounded the last corner and
there was the gate to the base. Mrs
Robinson drove in carefully and
pulled into the driveway of her house.
She helped Kate out of the car while
Drew picked up their bags and Kate's
skates. They walked across the grass,
Mrs Robinson holding Kate's hand,
and through the trees to the twins'

own house.

Although they were a lot earlier than expected, Dad was home and working in the garden. He looked up as they came towards the house.

"Hello, you're home early," he

called. "Did you get tired of skating?"

Kate started to cry and ran to Dad.

"What's the matter?" he asked softly.

Drew hung his head and said quietly, "She's broken her new front tooth." Then he looked up at Dad and said, "She's really good on skates Dad, and she can do really difficult things. But she just slipped. I was watching."

"Is that right, Kate?" asked Dad, cuddling her. Kate didn't say anything, but she felt guilty because Drew was trying not to say how she'd been showing off.

"Well, let's look at the damage," said Dad.

They all trooped into the house.

Dad sat Kate on a chair in the kitchen and knelt beside her. He carefully held Kate's mouth open while he looked at the tooth.

"Oh dear," he sighed, "you have made a mess of it. Drew, did you look for the missing piece?"

Drew nodded.

Dad turned back to Kate and held her hands. "Now listen. I'm not going to ask you what really happened now because you are hungry and frightened, and no doubt very sore. I don't think one night will do too much damage. But in the morning I want to know how you came to slip. I will ring the dentist now and make an appointment for tomorrow. I'll take the day off work."

Kate nodded, the tears trickling down her cheeks.

"Do you think the dentist might be able to cap the tooth?" asked Mrs Robinson, when Dad came back from telephoning. "I don't know," Dad replied. "He said to bring Kate over first thing tomorrow."

Next morning Kate ached all over. Her head hurt, and her mouth felt twice as big as ever. Drew took Kate out to the car and they buckled themselves in and waited for Dad to drive them to the dentist.

"Kate," said Dad as they were driving to Nowra, "can you tell me what happened yesterday?"

The tears came to Kate's eyes again. "I was being silly," she whispered. "I thought I could do a single-axel jump and turn around in the air, but I couldn't and I slipped. My skates rolled away and I hit my face on the floor."

Dad was quiet for a moment. "That wasn't very sensible, was it?"

"No," said Kate softly.

Dad drove past their school and parked just around the corner near the shops. They walked down the street to the dentist's surgery and went inside.

Drew stayed in the waiting-room and read a comic. Dad went into the surgery with Kate. Drew waited and waited. He looked at the clock and sighed. It didn't seem that the hands were moving at all. He finished reading the comic and started on the magazines. After nearly an hour Kate came out, with Dad behind her, and the dentist behind him. They were all smiling, even Kate. And as well as bruises and scratches she had a whole front tooth again!

"How did you do that?" asked

Drew in amazement.

"Well," said the dentist, "I've put a cap on it. It's a bit like a lid. But when Kate is twelve she will have to come back and have a proper cap fitted. This is only a temporary one. I can't do a proper one until she has all her second teeth."

"Wow!" said Drew. "That means she'll have that one for four years. Will it last that long?"

The dentist laughed. "Oh yes Drew, it'll last that long. In fact it might even last longer."

Dad said goodbye, thanked the dentist, and then they went outside. Kate felt very ashamed and guilty. She knew it cost a lot of money to go to the dentist.

Dad looked at her and smiled. "Cheer up," he said. "I think you've learned that showing off is not a good idea. I'm sorry you are so sore and that your mouth hurts, but at least you have a tooth again. Perhaps next time you are thinking about being a famous skater, you'll be more careful."

Chapter Six

Next morning Dad, Kate and Drew
set off early to drive to the airport to
meet Mum. The plane was on time so
they didn't have long to wait. Kate
saw Mum as she came out of the
customs door and ran to meet her,
with Drew following close behind.

They all hugged each other, then
Mum stood back and looked at them.

"I've only been away one week, but
I'm sure you've both grown," she
said.

46

Drew and Kate grinned at her.

"Kate!" said Mum with surprise. "You've got a new front tooth. Isn't it beautiful?"

The twins looked at each other and giggled. Wait till they told Mum about that tooth. She would be angry about Kate's silly behaviour, but she would be pleased that the dentist had been able to cap the tooth.

"Come on," said Dad. "Let's go home and talk about what we've all been doing."

When they reached home Mum put the kettle on and they all sat down at the table to have a cup of tea and a talk. Dad told Mum about the work he had done in the garden, and Mum told them a little about the conference

she had been to. Then she turned to
Drew and Kate.

"And what have you been doing
while I've been away? Did you go to
some exciting places with Mrs
Robinson?"

Kate hung her head and Drew
looked out of the window.

"What's this?" said Mum. "Is there
something I should know?"

Dad looked at Kate and said, "Do
you want to tell Mum yourself, or
shall I do it?"

"I broke my tooth," said Kate. "I
was showing off at the skating rink
and I fell over. But the dentist says it
will be all right if I'm careful."

Mum looked puzzled. "But you
have a new tooth. When I left you had

48

four gaps, now you have three and a new tooth. So which tooth did you break?"

"I broke my new tooth," said Kate, "and the dentist put a cap on it."

Mum looked at Dad who shook

his head. He felt Kate had suffered enough and now she needed Mum to be a bit sympathetic. Mum reached across and touched Kate's hand. "You are a silly girl sometimes, aren't you?" she said softly. "I suppose I should be angry, but I'm relieved that you weren't badly hurt. You must have bruises everywhere. When did it happen?"

"The day before yesterday," said Drew. "Mrs Robinson drove us to the rink after breakfast and we were going to stay all day. But we came straight home after Kate hurt herself. Then yesterday Dad took Kate to the dentist. They were ages, and I waited for them and read a comic."

"You really love skating, don't you

Kate?" said Mum. "But how can we help you improve so you don't fall over?"

Kate sat and looked at the table-top. Then she said, "My skates are too small, and because they are sneakers they don't hold my ankles like proper skates do. I was trying to turn in the air. If my skates had jump bars and proper bearings they would stop faster and it would be a bit easier."

Mum looked at Dad and then said, "Go outside and play now for a while. I'll call you in when lunch is ready."

Kate and Drew went outside. Kate sat on the swing and Drew kicked a football around the grass. They waited, knowing they had been sent

outside so Mum and Dad could talk.
Drew felt bad because he knew how
much Kate liked to skate, and Kate
felt bad because she knew it was
mostly her own fault that she had
fallen over.

Soon Mum came to the door and
called them in. They sat around the
table again while Dad served up their

soup. He put the pot down and looked at them both.

"Mum and I have had a talk," he said, "and we think you've learnt your lesson, Kate. Now, if you promise to be sensible about skating at the rink and around the footpaths,

we'll buy you a new pair of proper leather skates for your birthday. Also, I'll ask the Captain if a very small part of the car-park can be fenced off so that all the children have somewhere flat to play ball games and skate. But you must be very careful. Now, before you get too excited, there's something else. Skating by yourself won't be much fun, so Drew, you can have a pair of roller-skates too. They won't be as good as Kate's, but it will mean you can skate around together."

Kate and Drew grinned at each other. Kate thought it was too good to be true! Somewhere flat to skate where she could practise, and new skates as well. Drew thought about playing football on land where the ball didn't roll downhill. He also thought about playing hockey on roller-skates.

"Thanks!" they shouted.

"We'll be careful," said Kate. "I don't want to break the rest of my new teeth. I promise not to try any jumps until I can skate properly with *both* feet on the ground."